Christmas, Aliens, Gargoyles and Everything-Just-Right

by Jack Kurtz

Baker's Plays
7611 Sunset Blvd.
Los Angeles, CA 90042
bakersplays.com

GENERAL PRODUCTION NOTES

These are "Readers' Theater" scripts. If you're unfamiliar with this format, it's relatively simple. The "readers" sit on stools, holding the scripts in loose-leaf notebooks, and presenting the story to the audience using only their voices and body postures, without movement around the stage, costumes, or sets. For the beginning director, a few hints are in order.

During narrative portions of the scripts, the readers should be focusing their eyes on the audience, since they are telling them a story. In "scenes" when readers are portraying characters speaking to each other, those readers should have their eyes focused out over the heads of the audience. If two readers in a scene are supposed to be speaking to each other, they should each be focusing on a point above the heads of the audience, about ten feet in front of and midway between them. They should not actually look at each other.

Arrange the stools casually, not in a straight line. If possible, stools should be of different heights.

Be sure your cast works on projection. There's no point in doing the story if some of the audience can't hear the lines. Tell the cast to practice as if they were talking to someone in the back row.

Concentrate on cue pick-ups. Unless there is a reason for a pause, one line should follow immediately after the previous line, not even allowing time for a breath. I tell my readers and actors to get in the habit of taking a breath four or five words before the end of the line preceding theirs. This is particularly important in these scripts when sentences are broken in the middle.

Put plenty of life in the stories. Remember that your audience is at least partly children. Without getting sickeningly sweet or "talking down," emphasize ideas and emotions a little more than you might in a realistic presentation for adults.

Some readers play different characters within the same script. If possible there should be a clear change in voice.

I suggest that the children's roles be played by the youngest boy or girl you can find who is capable of reading the material reasonably well and who can be heard. All other roles should be played by adults, although Senior Highs could probably do them effectively.

Finally, purists do not call it Readers' Theater. It is "Interpreter's Theater," since, for the best production, it should not be read; it should be memorized. For one thing, it's hard to focus your eyes on anything but the page if the material is actually being read. However, for the original performance of these scripts we broke the rule. All of these scripts were first done without memorization and with a maximum of two rehearsals. Of course, this means the director has to have everything ready to go, but it makes it a lot easier to recruit readers around Christmas time. If you don't have you your cast memorize, be sure to have them hold their scripts high and look up as much as possible. You may choose how much of an effort you want to put into production. Even with the minimal effort we put in, a good time was had by all. I hope you'll have the same good time.

PRODUCTION NOTES for *Sara Elizabeth and the Everything-Just-Right Christmas.*

Nothing much needed here. When Reader 3 is playing Bob, he should have fun with the character – without overdoing it. During Sara's long speech about her plans for Christmas, the other readers should look at Sara (out over the audience – see General Notes –) and react in character, being careful not to draw attention away from Sara. Toward the end, when Sara opens the door, the reader should move her head as though peeking around the door.

PRODUCTION NOTES for *Timmy and the Christmas Strangers.*

This play deviates from traditional readers' theater by having the actors leave their stools at one point to (mostly) pantomime the action. Props needed are a set of earphones and a realistic-looking toy handgun. When the plane "lands" in Denver, after Reader 2's line "And they did," the readers lower their heads while a stagehand hangs two signs somewhere on the stage: "Denver International Airport" and "MEN." If no wall is handy, use coat racks or just the backs of chairs. The "MEN" sign must be placed a short distance to the side of the stools, not behind, to allow for effective blocking of the scene. Also, feel free to change the video game names to whatever is popular at the time of production.

PRODUCTION NOTES for *Christmas and the Gargoyle and the Big, Big Present.*

This play is a sequel to *Christmas and the Gargoyle Who Wouldn't Say Thank You*, published by Baker's Plays in *Gargoyles, Plastic Balls, and Soup: Readers' Theater Scripts for Christmas*. As in the earlier play, Reader 2 should speak in the voice of a "crochety old man" when he is portraying Mr. Magruder. Some suggestions on how to be a gargoyle: when the script calls for "gargoyle faces," readers should make their hands into claws, put them right up next to their cheeks, and arrange their faces into the most monstrous grimaces possible. Work on this. The children in the audience get a kick out of it.

PRODUCTION NOTES for *Timmy and the Alien.*

The "window" needed for this production can be any sort of low wall behind the stools. The choir rail will do if you're using the chancel for the production. Or use long tables on their sides and covered with "wallpaper." The only prop needed is a red Santa hat. Use your imagination when creating makeup for the Alien. He should be "different" enough to cause the screaming, perhaps even green with pointy ears! He should speak in a strange voice, noticeably different from "humans."

SARA ELIZABETH AND THE EVERYTHING-JUST-RIGHT CHRISTMAS

THE CAST

READER 1 (Who also plays **SARA**)
READER 2 (Who also plays **MOM**)
READER 3 (Who also plays **BOB**)
READER 4 (Who also plays **DAD**)

SETTING

The setting is a bare stage or chancel with four stools for the "readers." For further details on production, see the PRODUCTION NOTES at the front of the book, both the general notes and the specific notes for this script.

READER 1. Sara Elizabeth Armbruster Burke

READER 2. Was a nice little girl with just one funny quirk.

READER 3. She was pleasant and pretty and reasonably bright,

READER 4. But she always insisted that things be "just right."

READER 2. While most other mothers had to beg and implore

READER 1. Their sons and their daughters to close the back door,

READER 4. And fathers quite often got red in the face

READER 3. When they saw children's toys spread all over the place;

READER 4. While other kids threw all their clothes on the floor,

READER 1. And had bedrooms that looked just like countries at war,

READER 3. While they dawdled at dressing and made their folks late,

READER 2. While they toyed with the spinach that sat on their plates,

MOM. My Sara's room sparkled from ceiling to floor,

DAD. And she ate all her vegetables, then asked for more.

MOM. She made her bed daily before it got light,

READERS 1-4. For Sara thought everything should be "just right."

MOM. She always hung all her clothes on their hangers,

DAD. Arranged by the colors, just one inch apart,

MOM. She kept all her "undies" in drawers out of sight,

READERS 1-4. For Sara thought everything should be "just right."

READER 1. There was one little problem in all this perfection,

READER 2. For she held an opinion that did cause some friction:

SARA. "If I'm always 'just right' in the things that I do,
I don't see why others can't be 'just right,' too."

READER 3. So she scolded her mother if the tables weren't dusted,

READER 4. And griped at her father when the TV was busted,

READER 2. And corrected the grammar of all that she knew,

SARA. "I'm sure that they all want to be 'just right,' too."

READER 1. She lived her whole life seeking errors to catch,

READER 3. And she often told classmates their clothes didn't match.

READER 4. She pointed out all of the problems and spots

READER 2. In the lives of her friends…

BOB. Though she didn't have lots.

MOM. She picked up the litter she found in the street,

BOB. And she even picked lint off of strangers she'd meet.

READER 3. The whole world was messy, there was so much to do,

READER 4. But at least she could straighten out people she knew.

READER 1. Now the target of Sara's crusade for perfection,

READER 2. Who got most of her somewhat unwelcome attention,

READER 4. Was her brother, a likable fellow named Bob,

READER 3. Who was sometimes called "careless,"

READER 4. but more often, "slob."

MOM. His bedroom lay deep with his clothes where he'd drop them,

DAD. With airplanes and ball bats lying atop them.

READER 4. It looked like the place where a comet had plopped,

READER 3. Or a big garage sale where a bomb had been dropped.

MOM. When told to be home before five from his play,

DAD. Bob thought he'd done well if he made it that day.

MOM. To match colors of shirts with his pants was a bother;

DAD. He thought he'd done well if his socks matched each other.

MOM. Sara coaxed him and shouted, she screamed and she pleaded,

SARA. "He will ruin my life if my warnings aren't heeded.
I try to be 'just right,' but what can I do
If the family I'm stuck with is not 'just right,' too?"

(Bob reacts in character.)

MOM. "She's my little perfectionist,"

READER 3.   Mommy would cry.

READER 1. "Why can't YOU be just like her,"

READER 2.   Other parents would sigh.

READER 4. "She's a little 'compulsive,'

READER 3.   Her teachers would warn,

READER 2. But old brother Bob heard it all with some scorn;

BOB. "You say that she's tidy and very fastidious,
But if you had to live here you'd soon learn to pity us.
Sara Elizabeth Armbruster Burke
May be all of that stuff...but she's mostly a jerk!"

* *

READER 1. On the fifteenth of August, while getting a tan,

READER 2. Sara Elizabeth started her plan

READER 3. For a "just perfect" Christmas from morning 'til night,

READERS 1-4. On that special day surely all must be "just right."

MOM. She made up a list of the things she would do,

READER 3. And wrote down a list for her family, too.

MOM. She announced that she'd scheduled the day so each minute

READER 3. Contained something special with "merriness" in it:

SARA. "At precisely 6:30 we'll all rise and shower,
And put on our clothes – that should take just an hour.

BOB. "OUR CLOTHES?!"

READER 1.   Shouted Bob,

BOB.   "Before opening one present?!"

SARA. "In that ratty old bathrobe you look like a peasant."

SARA. "Now so Mom will have all of the time that it takes,
She'll shower first, then fix juice and pancakes."

BOB. "WE'RE GOING TO EAT BREAKFAST BEFORE WE OPEN THE PRESENTS?!!!!!!!!!!!!!!

MOM. "PANCAKES?!!!!!!!!!"

SARA. "And then at 8:30, when the dishes are done,
We'll open the presents, two minutes for each one."

BOB, MOM, & DAD. "WASH THE DISHES?!!!!!!!!!!!!!!!"

(Sara remains unconcerned about her family's reactions)

SARA. "For gifts, I've made up a list, with the total right here.
It's five dollars more than my gift list last year.
For the increase you should see the clear explanation;
We all must allow for a little inflation.

"Now then,
When we've put all the wrappings in boxes and barrels,
It should be 10:30 and time for the carols,
Which we'll sing 'round the piano to brighten the day.
Mom will type out the words and I'm going to play.

"And then at eleven we'll all take a break,

While Mom heads to the kitchen to cook and to bake.
We'll stack up our presents and when that's all done,
We all should be ready for dinner at one.

"I'm baking plum pudding to finish the meal,
And when it's all eaten and dishes washed, we'll
Go off to a movie by Disney at two.
We'll be home by five and then here's what we'll do...."

READER 2. You get the idea, there's more if you care;

READER 4. It was Sara's great dream,

BOB. And her family's nightmare.

MOM. In the months before Christmas, she planned and she toiled,

READER 1. It would all be "just right," not a thing would be spoiled.

READER 2. On the day before Christmas it snowed in the night,

READERS 1-4. Adding just the right weather to make everything "just right."

READER 1. Well...

READER 2. They arose at 6:30 before it was dawn,

READER 3. But when Bob hit the shower the hot water was gone.

BOB. AAAAAARGH!!!!

READER 4. Therefore, fifteen long minutes were shot,

READER 1. So the pancakes were cold and the orange juice hot.

READER 2. When they opened the presents, poor Sara's lip trembled,

READER 3. For the blouse that she got only vaguely resembled

READER 4. The one she'd requested, though Mother explained,

MOM. "The store was sold out,"

READER 3. She couldn't be blamed.

READER 1. After all of the opening and thanking was done,

READER 4. Sara had all that she'd asked for, excepting one:

READER 3. A fine china doll with a rose covered hat,

READER 2. And Bob, looking puzzled, said,

BOB.   "I got you that."

BOB. "And I wrapped it myself with a big orange bow."

SARA. "Was the paper all wrinkled and yellow?"

READER 1. When Bob answered,

BOB.   "Yeah,"

READER 2.   Sara wailed in dismay,

SARA. "I thought it was trash and I threw it away!"

(Appropriate expressions from each character)

READER 1. Well, she finally recovered and sat down to play

READER 4. All the carols she'd planned on to brighten the
    day,

MOM. When the telephone rang, Dad answered the call,
    Then threw on his coat and ran out through the hall.

READER 1. Sara's dad was a doctor, you know, a physician –

READER 2. The kind that brings babies, a fine obstetrician.

READER 4. And he still wasn't back when Mom, dinner
    announced,

READER 3. And when Sara served plates of her pudding, it
    bounced.

READER 2. When Dad wasn't back at the time for the show,

READER 3. Her mother said,

MOM.   "Sara, we simply can't go."

READER 4. And since all of the things had gone wrong that
    she'd tried,

READER 2. She just ran to her room, locked her door, and
    she cried.

SARA. "WAAAAAAAAAAAAAAAAAAAAAAAAAH!!!"

READER 4. When her father got home and her mother
    explained,

READER 3. Father went to her room and said,

DAD. "Sara?"

SARA. "WAAAAAAAAAH!!!"

DAD. "Sara, please open the door."

SARA. "WAAAAAAAAAAAAAAAAAAAAAAAAAH!!!!!"

DAD. "Sara Elizabeth Armbruster Burke, open the door right this minute or...
Or...or…by golly, young lady, I'll blow dust under it!"

READER 2. Sara sniffled, and, opening the door, showed her head.

READER 3. Daddy came in and sat down on her bed.

DAD. "That's better. Now I have something to say, and I want you to listen."

SARA. *(sniff, sniff)* "Yes, Daddy."

DAD. "And I'm too tired to make it rhyme."

SARA. "Yes, Daddy."

DAD. "Now you got most of the presents you wanted and we had a fine breakfast, and I'm sorry I missed dinner, but Mrs. Wallace had her baby and babies won't wait."

SARA. "Yes, Daddy."

DAD. "So what's all the fuss?"

SARA. *(sniffle)* "It wasn't perfect. Everything should be 'just right' on Christmas."

DAD. *(thinking a minute)* "Now where did you get that idea? Things certainly weren't 'just right' on the first Christmas."

SARA. *(snuffle)* "They weren't?"

DAD. "Of course not. Do you think Mary wanted her baby to be born in a stable?"

SARA. "I never thought about that."

DAD. *(looks pleased with himself)* "Well, I'm sure she didn't. Stables aren't good places to have babies at all. But somebody fouled up. Maybe Joseph just forgot to make the reservation at the inn, or didn't think they'd need one, but did Mary get mad at him because of that?"

SARA. "I guess not, Daddy."

DAD. "I don't know. Maybe she did. But, the baby was more important than where it was born , and Mary wouldn't have wanted to spoil everything just because a few of the details didn't work out. Besides, the most important thing about Christmas is that God came to us in Jesus to show us his love. Do you think he only came to people who were perfect?"

SARA. "I don't know. Didn't he?"

DAD. "Certainly not. He came because people WEREN'T perfect and needed his help. Nobody is perfect, Sara. Not even you."

SARA. "I'm not?"

DAD. "No. Your mother and I are very happy that you keep your room clean and are always on time and always eat your vegetables and plan things out ahead of time. Those are all very good things. But frankly, Sara, when you start expecting everyone else to do just what you want them to do and get mad at them when they aren't perfect, you're…uh…being a jerk. You're doing just what God doesn't want us to do. He doesn't want us to be always criticizing and looking down on other people. After all, he loves us, even when we aren't perfect."

SARA. "Oh."

DAD. "Sara, you aren't the only one who has problems with Christmas."

SARA. "I'm not?"

DAD. "No. Lots of boys and girls get so excited about Christmas that when some little thing goes wrong – when they don't get what they want or a toy get broken right away, they get upset just like you did. Lots of boys and girls – and even adults – think Christmas should be perfect. When it isn't, they can't enjoy the good things that do happen on Christmas. Isn't that just what you're doing?"

SARA. "I guess so, Daddy."

DAD. "Now if you'll get dressed real fast, we can still make the 5:00 movie."

READERS 1-4. And they did.

* * * * * * * * * * * * *

READER 1. Sara Elizabeth Armbruster Burke

READER 2. Was sometimes quite nice, and sometimes a jerk.

READER 3. We've told you her story as sort of a warning,

ALL. So, Merry Christmas to all. Have a good Christmas morning.

The End

CHRISTMAS AND THE GARGOYLE AND THE BIG, BIG PRESENT

THE CAST

READER 1 (Who is also **DAD**)

READER 2 (Who is also **MR. MAGRUDER**)

READER 3 (Who is also **GRANDMA**)

READER 4 (Who is always **TIMMY**)

SETTING

The setting is a bare stage or chancel with four stools for the "readers." For further details on production, see the PRODUCTION NOTES at the front of the book, both the general notes and the specific notes for this script.

READER 1. This is a sequel.

READER 4. Which means that it's sort of like another story but only because it's got a lot of the same people in it but it isn't exactly like the same story because the people do different things.

READER 2. The trouble with a sequel is that not everybody has heard the first story and they don't know the people.

READER 4. So we have to do an "ASYOUWILLREMEMBER."

READER 2. A what?

READER 4. An "ASYOUWILLREMEMBER" like in Soap Operas. On Radio.

READER 3. When did you ever hear a radio soap opera?

READER 4. My Dad's got a couple of records. They're neuralgia records.

READER 1. Nostalgia records.

READER 4. That's what I said. Anyhow, the announcer says "ASYOUWILLREMEMBER in last week's episode, Helen Trent did something or the other." Which is silly, because if people remember you don't have to tell them. Really, it's for people who didn't hear last week or don't have very good memories at all. Anyhow, we're going to do an ASYOUWILLREMEMBER.

READER 3. As you will remember, in the first Gargoyle story we met Timmy.

READER 4. That's me.

READER 3. He lived in the Maple Heights Subdivision with his mother and father and grandmother and the Gargoyle.

READER 4. Except the Gargoyle didn't live in our house. He lived in a big old house right in the middle of all the little new houses in the Maple Heights subdivision, and his real name was Mr. Magruder.

READER 3. And Timmy and all of the children in the subdivision called him the Gargoyle because on the front of his big, old house were four little heads made of stone that stuck out and they all looked like monsters. They looked like this:

(**READERS** *make Gargoyle faces.*)

READER 1. But Timmy's father explained that all they really were were downspouts and the water ran off the roof over them and it had been doing it for a long time and they all had green streaks on their faces, like this:

(**ALL FOUR** *run fingers down faces like streaks.*)

READER 2. The stone heads were called Gargoyles, and because, one day, Mr. Magruder came out and yelled at Timmy and his friends for playing in his garden, and he looked mad, like this:

(**READER 2** *makes face.*)

READER 4. And he had his hair running down his face, like this:

(**READER 2** *runs fingers down his face.*)

READER 3. After that, Timmy and his friends called him the Gargoyle.

READER 4. But his real name was Mr. Magruder.

READER 2. And the first story was about how the Gargoyle always yelled at all the children when they played in his garden and how Grandmother persuaded Timmy to give the Gargoyle a Christmas present.

READER 4. Two Christmas presents.

READER 3. One of them doesn't count. You owed Mr. Magruder a rose bush to replace the one you tore up.

READER 4. Okay, but anyhow, the Gargoyle…

READER 1. Mr. Magruder.

READER 4. Mr. Magruder didn't say thank you for either of the Christmas presents, and Grandma explained to me that God still loved us even though we threw away lots of his gifts and that's called a Moral and that was what the first Gargoyle story was about. Only there was more, but we won't tell you that or we won't have time to tell you this story.

READER 1. The children didn't start to notice anything different until in the spring.

READER 3. Then one day, when they were playing in Mr. Magruder's garden…

READER 4. Which wasn't really a garden but used to be and there wasn't anything to tear up because everything got all messy a long time ago.

READER 3. One day when the children were playing, one of the boys saw Mr. Magruder peeking out the window, around the curtain, like he didn't want them to see him.

READER 4. So we all ran and hid because we didn't want the Gargoyle to yell at us – but then somebody got to thinking. The Gargoyle hadn't come out and yelled at us since last Christmas. Not ever. And so we snuck back and peeked and the Gargoyle was still at his window peeking out, trying to see us, but he wasn't out on his porch yelling like he used to. We thought maybe he was sick.

READER 2. And the next time when the children played in the garden, he didn't come out again, but they saw him peeking.

READER 1. And the next time, too.

READER 4. But the third time…

READER 2. Boy!

READER 4. He was standing there on the porch pointing right at me.

READER 2. Boy! Come here a minute.

READER 4. Not again. I hadn't even torn up a rose bush this time. I didn't think I had anyhow.

READER 2. Boy! Come here.

READER 4. Yes, sir?

READER 2. You're the boy that tore up my rose bush last Christmas, aren't you?

READER 4. Yes, sir. But we bought you a new one. Remember?

READER 2. Uhuh. I threw it away.

READER 4. Yes, sir.

READER 2. You brought me a Christmas Tree, too. Right?

READER 4. "Yes, sir." I wish he'd just kept quiet about that. All the other kids were lookin' at me funny.

READER 2. Never had a chance to thank you for it. (*pause.*) Thank you.

READER 1. The Gargoyle turned on his heel and went back in the house.

READER 3. And for another month they didn't see him…

READER 1. And then one day, when the weather was really nice, and they were all playing war dodging in and out of the old hedgerows and bushes in the Gargoyle's reined garden, the Gargoyle came out on the porch again.

READER 2. Boy! Come here a minute.

READER 4. We're sorry sir. We'll get off your property.

READER 2. You can stay. You can't hurt anything in the garden that nature didn't "do in" decades ago. I just want you to see something. Bring your friends.

READER 3. Somewhat reluctantly they approached the Gargoyle's back porch. The Gargoyle held a strange, hat-like object in his hand.

READER 2. Playing war?

READER 4. Yes, sir.

READER 2. Thought so.

READER 1. He held up the object.

READER 2. Ever see anything like that?

READER 4. No, sir.

READER 2. What do you suppose it is?

READER 4. It looks kind of like a hat.

READER 2. It's a helmet. From the Great War. World War I. German helmet.

READER 4. Were you a German back then?

READER 2. (*Snorts, almost a laugh*) No, boy. I was an American. Even way back then. Fought for America. Just found this helmet. I thought…I thought you might like to see it.

READER 1. And with that he turned on his heel and marched back into the house.

READER 4. It looked sort of like a helmet, but it had a real fancy point on the top. Maybe they didn't have guns back then, so they just lowered their heads and ran at each other.

READER 3. From then on when the children played in the garden, the Gargoyle would come out of the house and sit and watch them, and sometimes even smile.

READER 1. And sometimes he'd bring something out to show them.

READER 4. One time it was a great big sword and another time a stero-optician.

READER 1. Stereopticon.

READER 4. That's what I said. Anyhow, that's like a real old Viewmaster, except each card has just two big pictures and they're brown and the people have on funny old-time clothes.

READER 3. One day in the summer, the Gargoyle even came over and knocked on Timmy's door and wanted to know if he'd like to earn a little money, and so Timmy spent a little time digging up around the Gargoyle's old roses…and a few of them even bloomed again.

READER 1. And finally came Christmas…or about a month before Christmas, when the postman made a mistake.

READER 2. Over on the other side of the city from Timmy's suburb of Maple Heights with its little houses close together was the suburb of Maple Hills with great big houses that weren't close together at all.

READER 3. And one morning when Timmy's father was sorting through their mail he found a catalogue from Arbor's Department Store addressed to Boxholder,

Maple Hills. Now Timmy's family got catalogues from Penney's, and L.L. Bean and Land's End, but only people in Maple Hills got catalogues from Arbor's Department store.

READER 4. My mom says they just sell mink bathrobes and diamond water faucets and stuff. But since there wasn't any way we could return mail to somebody named Boxholder, we just kept the catalogue. And my dad would look through it, and every once in a while he'd chuckle a little. But sometimes when he chuckled he looked sort of sad.

READER 3. Then one night when Timmy was lying on the couch watching television and he was too lazy to go to his room to get one of his comic books, he picked up the catalogue out of the magazine rack and looked at all the stuff on all the pages and wondered why anybody would want most of it or why anybody would pay that much for a bunch of cheese wrapped in fancy paper until he came to a page where....

READER 4. Oh Boy! Oh Boy! Oh Boy!

READER 2. It was called the Indianapolis 498, which Dad said was kind of a joke. It was a red racing car with flames painted down the sides and it was ten feet long…just the right size for Timmy…and it ran on a motor sort of like one in a lawnmower.

READER 4. Oh Boy! Oh Boy! Oh Boy!

READER 3. And it cost…

READER 1. (*Incredulously*) TWENTY-ONE HUNDRED AND FORTY-SIX DOLLARS AND THIRTY-TWO CENTS! Timmy, I could buy a real car for that. You know we can't spend that much on Christmas.

READER 4. I wouldn't want anything else at all for Christmas. Not even candy in my stocking.

READER 1. Even if we could afford it, boys your age shouldn't have presents like that.

READER 4. I wouldn't want anything else for the next four Christmases.

READER 1. Timmy, you're just being ridiculous.

READER 4. And I knew it. But that didn't keep me from wishing.

READER 2. So Timmy carried the catalogue everywhere he went, and it go so that the catalogue just automatically fell open to the page with the Indianapolis 498 Junior Racer.

READER 4. And that's how the Gargoyle happened to see it. It was the second time he'd ever come to my house.

READER 2. Mrs. Murchison. I have a favor to ask of you.

READER 4. Mrs. Murchison is my Grandmother. She has a different name from me because she's my mother's mother and when mothers marry fathers they get the same name as the father, which my Grandmother says is wrong and they won't be doing it that way in a few more years, but I hope they do because if there were two Mrs. Murchisons in our house we wouldn't know who to call to the phone.

READER 2. I'm going away for awhile.

READER 4. I'd never seen the Gargoyle look so happy.

READER 2. Visiting my grandson over the holidays. Be leaving in about a week. Flying. Anyhow, I'd like to give you the key to my house. In case there's a fire or anything.

READER 4. And about that time I walked in…with my catalogue.

READER 2. What's that, Timmy?

READER 4. Just a catalogue.

READER 2. And what are you getting for Christmas?

READER 4. Probably just some socks and underwear and dumb things like that.

READER 1. But Mr. Magruder leaned down and looked at the catalogue and the Indianapolis 498, and then he looked at the price, and he smiled.

READER 4. Mr. Magruder smiles now. Actually, he smiles a lot. I don't know how he learned since a year ago.

READER 2. Well, that's quite a bit for a young man like you.

I doubt whether most young men should have that kind of a present. It might cause them to miss some of the important things in life.

READER 4. Which was pretty much what my dad had said, and my mother, and my grandmother. I think adults get together and work out what to tell kids.

READER 3. And then Mr. Magruder left.

READER 1. But that night, when Timmy was supposed to be in bed – and he was, except that he had a comic book and his flashlight under the covers – he heard Mr. Magruder downstairs talking to his parents.

READER 2. I'll be leaving in a week, but I've made arrangements for a present for Timmy to be delivered here a short time before Christmas. I know very well what you'll say about it, that it's too big and too expensive. Well, I want to do it. Your son gave me more last Christmas than any of you will ever know. This is my way of finally saying "Thank you."

READER 4. A big present! An expensive present! It had to be....

READER 3. On December 23rd Timmy's present was delivered. It was big all right.

READER 4. It took two trucks.

READER 1. The first truck carried a package wrapped in green, waterproof plastic with a red plastic bow and a great big sticker that said Do Not Open until Christmas.

READER 4. The second truck *was a crane.*

READER 2. The man in the truck with the crane put chains very carefully around the present and very carefully the crane set the present down in Timmy's yard.

READER 3. The present was six feet square....

READER 2. And twelve feet high.

READER 1. Uh, pardon me, but are you sure you haven't got it setting on the wrong end?

READER 2. I got my instructions, Mac. They said set it down just the way it was on the truck.

READER 3. Timmy's father looked puzzled.

READER 1. Well, maybe that's the way they pack it.

READER 4. All day all the other kids came by and just stared at my present. I know I shouldn't have, but I told them what it was.

READER 2. All the kids started being very nice to Timmy. They all wanted to be the first to ride in his race car.

READER 3. People driving by remarked on what a large lawn decoration it was.

READER 4. It was a Big, Big present.

READER 2. Christmas morning.

READER 3. Oh, let him open it first, Fred. He won't pay any attention to the other presents if he doesn't.

READER 1. He won't pay any attention to the other presents if he does.

READER 2. But Timmy's father, who looked a little sad because he knew that he couldn't get Timmy anything as nice as a race car, went down into the basement and got a crowbar and after the paper was more or less off, he started to pry the boards off the big, wood box.

READER 4. I started feeling sick just as soon as the first board came off. Whatever was inside was shaped funny and it wasn't red…it was gray.

READER 1. And Timmy felt sicker and sicker every time another board came off. And when the last board came off, everybody just stared and Timmy ran in the house crying. It was…

READER 2. …a statue.

READER 3. It was a man, who looked as if he had just started to get up out of a chair and he was reaching up for something.

(**READER 2** *assumes position*)

READER 4. And he didn't have any clothes on, and he looked like he was trying to grab at some bunch of pigeons. Maybe the pigeons stole his clothes and were flying off with them. And he was even broken. He didn't have a thumb on one hand. (**READER 2** *closes thumb*) I guess the pigeons had bitten it off.

READER 1. Grandma went in the house and brought Timmy back out.

READER 3. Now, Timmy, I know it isn't what you wanted, but it's really a very fine statue. It's probably the nicest thing Mr. Magruder owned, and he wanted to give it to you, and that shows that he appreciates what you did for him last Christmas, very much.

READER 4. But even Grandmother sounded a little funny, and I could tell that all three of them were wondering what they were going to do with an eleven-foot statue in the front yard.

READER 2. Well, Timmy went in and opened his other gifts and there was a camera and a back pack and really a lot of nice stuff to go along with the underwear and socks, and Timmy stopped pouting, – well, almost, – but it wasn't much of a Christmas.

READER 1. The next day Timmy's father called the museum. He said he couldn't see how they could keep a statue that size in their front yard, and maybe they could "loan" it to the museum if it was good enough for them to take, maybe to fill up a space in one of the back rooms or something, or maybe put outside in the park.

READER 3. And a funny little man came out from the museum, looking bored, but when he saw the statue he stopped looking bored, and he started running all around the statue, looking at it real close, and he even climbed up in its lap, and looked at the hand missing the thumb.

READER 2. Can't tell you anything until I check some records, sir. Could you come to my office tomorrow afternoon at two?

READER 3. And Dad went, and when he came home he sort of looked like one of those people on television, right after they've seen one of the Munsters.

READER 1. When Mr. Magruder was rich he used to collect works of art. When he lost his money, apparently he sold everything but this statue.

READER 4. Mr. Magruder lost most of his money in something called the repression.

READER 1. The curator of the museum figures he must have it stored somewhere all these years. It's....

READER 4. Dad made a kind of strangling noise.

READER 1 ...an original Rodan. The curator said it wasn't one of his better works. It was probably worth only... about...$400,000.

READER 4. Well, we loaned the statue to the museum until Mr. Magruder got back, and then my folks tried to talk Mr. Magruder into taking the statue back, but he wouldn't do it because he said I'd given him his grandson back – which was part of last year's story – and that a grandson was worth a lot more than a statue. Anyhow, he said that maybe later I'd want to sell it and it could pay for my college education and stuff, and Mom cried because she said now I could go to any college I wanted, which didn't excite me too much, because you don't need to go to college to be a fireman, but I guess the present was still something kind of special, even if it wasn't as special as a race car. You got a Moral, Grandma?

READER 3. Well, yes Timmy, I think I do. Sometimes the things we think we want aren't really the best presents after all. But we have to grow up to find out what the really good presents are. Sometimes your Mom and Dad, because they love you, won't give you something because they know you really wouldn't like it after you got it, or because they know it wouldn't be good for you, or because it really isn't good for anybody, children or adults, to have too many toys, because then they pay more attention to their toys than to really important things.

READER 4. That's why Mr. Magruder didn't get me the racer?

READER 3. I suppose.

READER 4. You didn't say anything about God.

READER 3. You didn't give me time. What do you suppose the Shepherds would have asked for if they'd known God was going to give them a gift?

READER 4. Probably more sheep or a nicer house or something.

READER 3. Probably. And if God had given them that, it wouldn't have been anywhere near as nice as what he did give them. But I still wonder if the shepherds weren't just a little disappointed. I know you learn in Church School that Jesus is the most important gift we get at Christmas, but, now be honest with me Timmy, do you really get as excited at Christmas about Jesus as you do about the other presents?

READER 4. I try to.

READER 3. But do you?

READER 4. Well...I guess not.

READER 3. Well, it's just like the statue. You need to grow up and learn things before you'll realize how really beautiful the statue is and how important college is. The more you understand, the more you'll realize what a wonderful gift Mr. Magruder gave you. It's the same thing with Jesus. We have to grow up, really grow up, not just get bigger. Then we start to realize how much more important that gift is than any other.

READER 4. Okay. Well, that's this year's story. This spring my class went to the Museum and I got to show all the kids my statue. I mean, it really isn't a bad looking statue. Boy, could that guy have played football. But I guess I still don't really understand why it's such a beautiful statue. My Grandma says someday I'll understand it. Mostly, I'm just curious about one thing. I wonder where the pigeons took his clothes.

The End

TIMMY AND THE CHRISTMAS STRANGERS

THE CAST

READER 1 (Who also plays **DAD**)

READER 2 (Who also plays **GRANDMA**)

READER 3 (Primarily narration)

READER 4 (Who also is the **FEDERAL MARSHALL**)

TIMMY

READER 5 (Who also is the **TEENAGE GIRL** wearing earphones)

READER 6 (Primarily narration, but actor should look like she could be
a grandmother)

READER 7 (Who also is the **GANG MEMBER**)

SETTING

The setting is a bare stage or chancel with eight stools for the "readers."
For further details on production, see the PRODUCTION NOTES at the
front of the book, both the general notes and the specific notes for this
script.

READER 1. In October, Timmy's parents told him that they were going to move.

READER 2. Being a sensible young man, and quite mature for his age, Timmy took the news calmly.

TIMMY. NOOOOOOOOO! I DON'T WANNA MOVE! WAAAAAAAAAAAA!

READER 1. He pointed out to his father and mother that there were many intelligent reasons for not moving.

TIMMY. I'LL GET UP IN THE DARK TO GO TO THE BATHROOM AND I'LL FORGET I'M IN A NEW HOUSE AND I'LL FALL DOWN THE STAIRS AND BREAK MY NECK AND DIE!

READER 2. Mom explained that Dad had gotten a wonderful promotion in his job and they'd be living in a fine new neighborhood and that Timmy would be going to a fine new school.

TIMMY. THEY'LL HAVE DIFFERENT SCHOOL BOOKS AND DIFFERENT TEACHERS AND I'LL FLUNK!

READER 1. Dad pointed out that he'd make lots of new friends.

TIMMY. THEY'LL HATE ME AND BE JUVENILE DELINQUENTS AND HAVE GANGS AND THEY'LL TAKE ME OUT IN AN ALLEY AND BEAT ME UP AND I'LL DIE!!!

READER 2. But in November they moved anyhow.

TIMMY. You just can't reason with parents.

READER 3. And Timmy didn't fall down the stairs of his new house.

TIMMY. I fell down in my bedroom.

READER 2. Because you left your ice skates in the middle of the floor.

READER 7. And he didn't flunk.

TIMMY. But I got a "D" on my geography test 'cause we were studying Antarctica when I left and South America when I got there. They don't have any penguins in Brazil.

READER 6. And nobody beat him up.

TIMMY. They didn't hardly pay any attention to me at all. Except they laughed at me because I thought there were penguins in Brazil.

READER 5. Timmy really didn't make friends very fast at school.

READER 6. They did move into a fine new neighborhood, so fine that the people who lived there were mostly older than Timmy's parents and their children were older than Timmy or they were grown up and gone and there wasn't anybody at all to play with except Stanley.

TIMMY. Stanley the Strange.

READER 1. Timmy!

TIMMY. Well he is! He must weigh about two million pounds and he wears glasses that look weird and he breathes funny.

READER 1. He has asthma.

TIMMY. At least when he comes over to play I can hear him two houses away and hide.

READER 1. *(sternly)* Young man, you need to change your attitude.

TIMMY. I needed to change my home. Oh, gosh, I wanted to go back where we used to live.

READER 7. And on Christmas, they were going to do just that.

READER 6. Timmy's grandmother had just kept their old home when they moved.

TIMMY. She said she didn't want to leave all her friends. It worked for her.

READER 5. So on the 22nd of December they were all going to fly home and spend Christmas and a whole week afterward in their old house with Grandma.

TIMMY. And all my old friends will be there and it'll be great.

READER 4. And then.

READER 1. *(as Dad)* "Well, he's our biggest client and he wants your mother and me to come to a party at his house on the twenty-third. It's no big problem. We'll just fly out on Christmas Eve and get there late."

TIMMY. THAT'S TWO WHOLE DAYS!

READER 1. Timmy, I have to go to this party.

TIMMY. Skeeter Janowitz has to go to his grandparents' house for Christmas and stay a week afterward and I won't be able to see him at all.

READER 1. There's nothing we can do about it.

TIMMY. You promised we'd go on Wednesday.

READER 1. I know, but…Wait a minute. You're getting to be a big boy now. How would you like to fly by yourself? Mom and I could come up on the twenty-fourth, but you could go ahead on Wednesday and fly by yourself.

READER 2. And so that's what he did.

READER 4. They made arrangements with Grandmother to meet him at the airport, and they made arrangements with the airline so the attendant would know he was traveling alone and kind of keep an eye on him. And they took him to the airport, and waved goodbye when he got on the plane.

READER 3. Timmy had never been on a plane before in his life.

READER 7. He was really excited.

(Timmy is waving. **READERS 1 & 2** *begin a low whine as if jet engines are warming up.)*

READER 3. *(terribly bright and cheerful)* Good morning, ladies and gentlemen. We are taxiing out now to put ourselves in position for take-off. Please fasten your seatbelts. *(Demonstrates in pantomime.)* There are emergency exits located at the front of the plane and immediately over either wing. In the unlikely event that we should come down over water, your seat cushions also function as flotation devices. Should the plane experience a sudden depressurization, an oxygen mask will automatically drop from the ceiling above your seat. Place it over your nose and mouth in this fashion. *(Through all of this, TIMMY is becoming increasingly uneasy.)* I believe we're ready for take-off now, and I wish you all a pleasant journey.

READER 3. *(leaning over toward Timmy)* You Timmy?

TIMMY. Uh-huh.

READER 3. Yeah, well, I'll be keeping an eye on you. If you want anything, just let me know. Try not to want anything. I've gotta headache that could…

READER 7. And then…

> *(ALL READERS begin to make various noises that increase in pitch, indicating airplane heading down the runway. TIMMY's eyes widen. He clutches the sides of his seat and closes his eyes tight. Finally all readers look up as plane leaves runway and noises lessen.)*

TIMMY. *(finally opens eyes and looks out window)* I couldn't believe it. We were flying. I thought the plane was going to shake itself apart.

READER 1. Finally, Timmy managed to relax a little, and started to enjoy himself.

READER 2. The clouds all looked neat from on top.

READER 3. He read a magazine.

READER 4. And for a while, even though he was so excited, he went to sleep.

READER 5. When he woke up again the pilot was talking to them over the intercom.

READER 4 …and so runway conditions in Seattle will not allow us to land at this time.

TIMMY. *(eyes big)* Are we just gonna fly around up here forever?

READER 4. We will be landing, instead, at Denver, until we receive word that the runways have been cleared.

READER 2. And they did.

READER 7. After they sat around the terminal for awhile, a man came out and gathered them all together and said,

READER 1. I'm terribly sorry. It appears that there is little chance of the Seattle airport being cleared for landing before morning. You will be rebooked on a flight leaving early in the morning. If you wish to attempt to use alternate means of transportation, we'll make every effort to help you.

READER 3. So the attendant, who looked even grouchier than she had been on the plane, helped Timmy call his parents, and they decided it would be best for Timmy to just wait there.

READER 1. He had a motel room all to himself, and they had movies on the TV set, and it was really kind of fun, and in the middle of the night, Timmy woke up and the snow was coming down real hard.

READER 2. in great big flakes,

READER 3. blowing against the window.

READER 6. and Timmy really felt like Christmas.

READER 5. and he could hardly wait to see his Grandma and all his friends tomorrow.

READER 7. Except …

READER 1. *(smiling sickly)* Uh, I have some good news and some bad news. The good news is that the runway in Seattle is clear. The, uh, bad news is that due to the unexpected severity and duration of the snowfall last night, we, uh, can't get off the ground here in Denver. We're hoping to get off the ground sometime late this afternoon.

READER 3. So the attendant, looking grouchier, still, helped Timmy call his grandmother so she wouldn't worry, and then she showed Timmy a comfortable place to sit and play with his Game Boy.

READER 2. All day he played the video games, and watched the snow fall.

READER 5. He played Super Mario Brothers.

READER 2. And watched the snow fall.

READER 5. Finally he got so good that he rescued the princess seven times.

READER 4. And his hand hurt.

READER 2. And he watched the snow fall.

READER 5. And finally the snow didn't look like Christmas any more.

READER 1. It made him want to cry.

READER 7. And about supper time, the man from the airlines got up, looking even more miserable than before...

READER 1. We're, uh, really sorry about this, but this is the worst snowfall we've had in years and now none of the buses or trains are moving either and...

READER 6. And they spent another night in the motel and the movie on television was from France and had subtitles and all anybody did was stare at each other a lot.

READER 2. And it snowed.

READER 3. The next day at the airport the stewardess didn't even say good morning, just made sure Timmy had his video game with him and then stalked off through the waiting room.

READER 6. And it was Christmas Eve.

READER 2. And it snowed.

READER 5. Timmy switched to Pokeman.

READER 2. And it snowed.

READER 5. And finally Timmy just sat and watched the snow fall.

READER 1. And it was Christmas Eve.

READER 4. After supper the man from the airline got everybody together.

READER 1. We're almost sure that the snow is going to stop soon, and we're almost sure that we can get the runways cleared in time to get you to Seattle no later than tomorrow afternoon.

TIMMY. TOMORROW AFTERNOON. That's Christmas!

READER 3. And the man looked miserable again, and all the other people looked mad.

READER 6. So Timmy phoned his grandmother.

*(****READERS 1,3,4,5,6,7**** have their heads down, to indicate that they aren't in the following scene.* **READER 5** *puts on earphones.)*

TIMMY. Grandma, we aren't going to be there until tomorrow afternoon.

GRANDMA (READER 2). Oh. That's too bad, Timmy. Your Mom and Dad are coming a different route and they'll be in here tonight. Don't you worry. We won't open any presents before you get here.

TIMMY. But it's Christmas Eve and I'm gonna have to spend it without you or Mom and Dad or any of my friends, and I'm gonna wake up Christmas morning in this airport with no presents and nobody but strangers. *(He is close to crying.)*

GRANDMA. Good. You won't be alone on Christmas.

TIMMY. Wadda you mean? Of course I'm alone.

GRANDMA. There are all those other strangers on the plane.

TIMMY. Yeah, but I don't know any of them.

GRANDMA. A stranger is just a friend you haven't made yet.

TIMMY. Dad says Grandma talks like Ben Franklin, whatever that means. *(Pause)* Grandma, none of them have even talked to me, except the attendant, and all she does is grumble and hand me my Game Boy.

GRANDMA. I think you'll have to explain that to me later. Well, I'm sure if you'll be friendly to them, they'll be friendly to you.

*(****TIMMY**** looks over at the others. All except* **READER 5** *raise heads and look just as grouchy as possible.* **READER** *5 moves slightly, in time to the music.)*

TIMMY. Grandma, you've always been real good at giving advice, but I think this time you blew it.

GRANDMA. You try it.

TIMMY. Christmas is for being with friends.

GRANDMA. You know, I'm not so sure about that. Of course it's very nice if you can be with friends and family, but *we've* done that to Christmas. It certainly didn't start out that way.

TIMMY. What do you mean?

GRANDMA. Why the first Christmas was all about being with strangers. Joseph and Mary were a long way from home and they didn't know anyone, and when Jesus was born none of their friends were there to say congratulations, and they couldn't tell their relatives or anything. Only strangers came. Shepherds and maybe a few people from Bethlehem and the wise men came later, and none of them were their friends. You know, Jesus himself said that Christianity wasn't about loving your friends. Everybody does that. He didn't have to come to teach people that. He said the important thing was to love strangers…and even people you don't like…like Stanley the Strange.

TIMMY. How'd you know about him?

GRANDMA. *(mysteriously)* Grandmas know. Now go back and wish all those strangers a Merry Christmas. I think you'll find they're really very friendly people.

*(**READER 4** gets up, reaches for something in pocket, and accidently reveals a gun.)*

TIMMY. Grandma, uh, one of those friendly people is a criminal. He has a gun. I just saw it under his coat.

GRANDMA. My, you still have your imagination Timmy. It was probably a hearing aid or something. Now you just go over to all those strangers and wish them a Merry Christmas.

TIMMY. Yeah.

GRANDMA. And I'll see you tomorrow afternoon.

TIMMY. Yeah. Bye, Grandma.

GRANDMA. Merry Christmas.

TIMMY. Merry Christmas.

(All except girl with radio look at him sourly.)

READER 7. Yeah. *(All face front in boredom as* **TIMMY** *slumps down in his seat. After a while* **READER 7** *gets up and goes into "restroom.")*

READER 1. When Timmy saw the young man go into the restroom, that reminded him that maybe he ought to wash his hands, so…*(***TIMMY** *gets up and follows. As he goes through the door, the young man is pantomiming preparing a hypodermic needle.)*

READER 2. Timmy stared. The young man was about to "shoot heroin."

READER 4. *(opens door, pulls gun, and aims it at young man, over Timmy)* FREEZE!! I'M A FEDERAL MARSHALL.

READER 7. FREEZE YOURSELF. I'M A DIABETIC.

*(***TIMMY** *SCREAMS.)*

READER 4. Really?

READER 7. Here's my medical card.

*(***READER 4, L***ooks at card. Embarrassed, he heads back for seat. In a moment* **TIMMY** *follows, then young man.)*

READER 4. *(back in Reader mode)* Look son, I'm sorry. I saw your paraphernalia in your pack, and you kinda looked like…

READER 7. Like an addict. Right. All diabetics should wear three-piece suits.

TIMMY. What's a diabetic?

READER 7. It's a disease. You can't cure it, but you can control it with insulin. That's what was in the hypodermic needle.

TIMMY. I thought it was dope, like heroin or something.

READER 7. Yeah.

TIMMY. *(to* **MARSHALL***)* I thought you were a gangster. I saw your gun.

READER 7. See how easy it is to judge people too quickly?

READER 4. Yeah. Look, most of the people I deal with are rotten. I'm afraid you get to thinking everybody is. You just don't trust strangers.

TIMMY. My Grandma says a stranger is just a friend you haven't made yet. She says it's just like the first Christmas to be with a bunch of strangers, because Mary and Joseph were sort of stranded too.

READER 6. You're going to see your grandmother? I'm going to see my grandchildren. I have some pictures right here. *(She brings them out, and all lean toward her, as though they are looking at the photos.)*

READER 2. Well, that started it. She told all about her grandchildren, and the Marshall told all about various criminals he'd known. And the young man said he was going to be a rock singer.

READER 5. *(snatching off headphones)* YOU ARE?!!

READER 2. And all of Christmas Eve they talked and talked and talked, and they even sang some Christmas Carols. *(Girl replaces earphones and listens to music.)* Except after awhile, they all sort of wandered away, and Timmy was all alone with the girl with the radio. *(Except for* **TIMMY**, **READER 1** *and* **READER 2**, *all wander off stage.)*

READER 1. "The time is now midnight and we at the Denver International Airport want to wish you all a Merry Christmas." *(Leaves stage)*

READER 2. And then Timmy started feeling sad again, because he wasn't at Grandma's and all his new friends were gone, too. *(Leaves stage)*

TIMMY. *(Lifts* **READER 5**'s *earphone.)* Merry Christmas.

READER 5. Huh? *(sadly)* Oh, yeah.

TIMMY. *(pantomimes reaching in flight bag)* Look, ah, here. Merry Christmas. *(gives her present)*

READER 5. Hey, I can't take that. You got it for somebody else.

TIMMY. It's okay. It's just perfume for my Mom. After I got it I found the perfume I got her last year and it was still full.

READER 5. Hey, well, thanks. Merry Christmas. I don't have nothing with me for you.

READER 4. *(entering with others)* But we do. Merry Christmas, Timmy. *(resume places on stools)*

READER 1. And they all gave him presents, things they'd managed to find in their flight bags or around the airport.

READER 2. The Marshall gave him $5 with a note that said he should buy himself a puzzle book since he was tired of playing video games.

TIMMY. I asked him if it would be all right if I used the money for candy, and he said it would.

READER 1. The plane finally took off at 6:00 a.m. and they were actually in Seattle by 8:00 in the morning, but by the time Timmy got to Grandma's he was so sleepy they didn't open their presents until afternoon anyhow.

READER 2. Well, Timmy had a great time at Grandma's and with all his old friends.

READER 3. But when they got back to his new home, he remembered about strangers becoming friends and how it had really happened on Christmas Eve, and there wasn't anybody stranger than Stanley, so he stopped running when Stanley came over to play.

READER 4. And, doggone it, Stanley was really a pretty nice guy.

TIMMY. Sometimes a hypodermic needle or a gun or being fat and breathing funny just isn't that important.

READER 5. And it wasn't long before Stanley started introducing Timmy to all his other friends at school.

TIMMY. And he had a lot of friends, because he was really a nice guy.

READER 6. Also, it didn't hurt that Stanley had an older brother, Sterling...

TIMMY. Who weighs about ten zillion pounds and plays defensive end for the Los Angeles Raiders.

READER 7. So Timmy learned that Christmas wasn't just

about family and friends. It was about strangers, too. Maybe especially about strangers.

TIMMY. Except it's hard to be nice to strangers. If you're nice to them, they get to be friends, and I guess it doesn't count anymore. Well, I gotta go now. I gotta see Stanley. He's my best friend.

The End

TIMMY AND THE ALIEN

43

THE CAST

READER 1 (mostly narration)
READER 2 (who is also **DAD**)
READER 3 (who is also **GRANDMA**)
READER 4 (who is always **TIMMY**)
READER 5 (who is always the **ALIEN**)

SETTING

The setting is a bare stage or chancel with five stools for the "readers."
Some type of low wall is needed behind the stools. For further details
on production, see the PRODUCTION NOTES at the front of the book,
both the general notes and the specific notes for this script.

READER 2. When Timmy was nine years old, a terrible thing happened.

READER 1. Timmy decided that Christmas was getting boring.

TIMMY. Not the presents. I still like the idea of the presents.

READER 2. It wasn't so much that he didn't like Christmas. It's just that they did the same things every year and somehow they just weren't as exciting as they used to be.

TIMMY. Some of the things. I still like the presents.

READER 3. But there were a lot of other things about Christmas that Timmy was tired of.

READER 2. For one thing, he was tired of the dancing Christmas trees.

READER 1. Every year, Timmy and his Mom and Dad and Grandma got in the car and drove 150 miles to another city, and got out of the car, and went into this big gymnasium and sat on the bleachers.

READER 3. And then about fifty Christmas trees came out and danced.

TIMMY. Except they aren't really Christmas trees. There's women inside these long pointy costumes with pine branches tied to them.

READER 2. The Christmas trees would sway back and forth.

TIMMY. Then they'd march around the floor like the band at football games while a piano played Christmas Carols.

READER 3. It was a special program of the "German Women's Cultural Heritage Society," and they've done it every Christmas for fifty years.

TIMMY. And at the end they'd all sing some song called "O Tannen*bomb*" and wave little American flags.

READER 3. And Dad would say

READER 2. "I can remember when I was a boy. We always went to see the dancing Christmas Trees."

TIMMY. "O Tannenbomb" isn't about a bomb at all. It's German for Christmas Tree. I could never figure why they sang in German and waved American flags."

READER 2. It's one of the oldest and most unusual Christmas traditions in America. Two years ago they had it on national television.

TIMMY. Yeah, some fat guy came out and danced with the Christmas Trees. Somebody named Willard Scott or something.

READER 1. Timmy had decided the dancing Christmas Trees were boring, anyhow.

TIMMY. And driving 150 miles each way is really boring.

READER 3. But what really did it was the time the Christmas Trees were on television and Timmy was trying to find the bathroom after the program, and he happened to glance through a half open door and there was this bunch of old ladies with their Christmas tree hats off and their heads just sticking out of Christmas tree bottoms and they didn't seem very Merry.

READER 3. "I was the organizer this year. It's only natural that I danced next to Mr. Scott!"

READER 1. "Well, I've been cleaning up all the pine boughs in that whole gymnasium for fifteen years, and that ought to count for something."

READER 3. "There wouldn't be so many pine boughs to clean up if you didn't bump into so many people when you danced."

READER 1. "It wouldn't make any difference if you did a decent job of sewing on your pine boughs."

TIMMY. Grandma had a word for it.

READER 3. Disillusioning.

TIMMY. That means after I saw them arguing I couldn't imagine them as Christmas trees any more. Heck, I knew they weren't really Christmas trees back when I was seven.

READER 2. But that wasn't the only reason Timmy was tired of Christmas.

TIMMY. I was tired of going out and chopping down our own Christmas tree in the woods.

READER 1. Every year, Dad would say,

READER 2. "Well, Timmy, time to go out and get our tree. I remember when I was a boy and my Dad would take me out to the woods to get a tree."

TIMMY. So while other kids with rich parents went to the supermarket to get a Christmas tree, or took it out of a box and put it together, we went to the woods.

GRANDMA. Timmy's Dad was very particular about the tree.

READER 2. "How about that one."

TIMMY. *(teeth chattering)* Looks great.

READER 2. "No, not quite tall enough."

TIMMY. And then we'd walk on for about another mile.

READER 2. "How about that one?"

TIMMY. *(teeth chattering)* "That's a great tree, Dad."

READER 2. "No. This side over here has a hole in it."

TIMMY. Then we'd walk another mile.

READER 2. "Maybe that one."

TIMMY. *(teeth chattering)* "That's got to be the best looking Christmas tree in the whole world."

READER 2. "Oh, look. There's a bird's nest in it. Well, we wouldn't want to disturb the birds."

TIMMY. "Disturb them! Disturb them! I haven't felt my feet for an hour. Thirty minutes ago I lost my knees."

READER 1. Then there was the year of the great ice storm.

READER 3. Every tree was covered with ice an inch thick.

TIMMY. Did that stop Dad? Noooooooooo.

READER 1. They rented a tractor to pull a half-ton of Christmas tree out of the woods.

TIMMY. A supermarket Christmas tree we can't afford. A tractor we can afford.

READER 1. And they put the tree in the basement to melt.

TIMMY. It ruined my sleeping bag.

READER 2. It wouldn't have if you'd had it on the shelf where it belonged instead of on the floor.

TIMMY. You don't figure a Christmas tree's gonna flood your basement.

READER 1. And Timmy was tired of being a shepherd in the Christmas pageant at the church.

TIMMY. I know what the Bible means when it says the shepherds were "sore afraid." The shepherds were afraid because of the angels, and their knees were probably sore because they had to kneel on a hard stage floor for thirty minutes while some little second grader tried to remember to say, "let us go now even unto Bethlehem and see this thing which has come to pass."

READER 3. But the thing that Timmy was most tired of was...

READER 2. "Well, Timmy, time to go see Santa Claus...

TIMMY. Look, uh, Dad. I'm in the fourth grade now and...

READER 3. But Dad would start looking sort of sad....

TIMMY. Well, okay, maybe just this one more year.

READER 1. And they went to see Santa Claus.

TIMMY. Talk about embarrassing. I tried to stand next to some little kid in line so they'd think he was my brother and I was taking *him* to see Santa Claus.

READER 1. And then Timmy sat on Santa's lap.

TIMMY. Kids, I got a rule. Call it Timmy's law. When you sit on Santa's lap and he has to look up at you, you're too old to sit on Santa's lap.

READER 1. Anyhow, Timmy was tired of Christmas.

READER 3. He was tired of the dancing Christmas trees and he was tired of tramping through the woods and he was tired of being a shepherd and he was tired of sitting on Santa Claus's lap.

TIMMY. It was all bor-ing.

READER 2. Timmy was tired of Christmas.

TIMMY. Except the presents. I still liked the presents.

READER 1. And then he overheard Dad saying to Mom….

READER 2. "What I really like about Christmas is how much Timmy enjoys it. It's really a special time for him with the dancing Christmas trees and going to get our tree and going to see Santa Claus."

TIMMY. Dad's eyes really lit up when he said it.

READER 3. That's when Timmy finally figured it out.

TIMMY. I suspected it when I was eight. We were doin' all this stuff for Dad. So I talked to Grandma.

READER 3. You may be right, Timmy.

TIMMY. Well, then, why can't Dad sit on Santa's lap. Ask him for aftershave lotion or something.

READER 3. Well, I don't think your father actually wants to do any of these things for himself. But he remembers how much they meant to him when he was a little boy, and he wants you to enjoy them as much.

TIMMY. Should I tell him I don't? I mean, I don't! I mean, I don't want to spoil his Christmas.

READER 3. That's very considerate of you. I don't think I can tell you what to do. You'll just have to decide for yourself.

READER 1. So that night Timmy was lying in bed trying to decide what to do, when…(*Coming from behind the "wall", sound of sleighbells, then sounds of tapping like "reindeer hoofs."*)

TIMMY. (*looks at audience*) Oh, oh. Uh…sounds on the roof. Uh…sounds like "the prancing and pawing of each little hoof." I don't think I believe this.

READER 2. And the sounds marched across the roof. And then there was a kind of scrabbling sound.

READER 1. And a whoosh. And a bump.

READER 3. Right outside Timmy's window.

READER 2. And Timmy got out of bed, and…

*(A red Santa Claus hat appears above wall. Timmy gets off stool to look toward the "window." **READERS 1, 2, &** **3** lower heads.)*

TIMMY. *(following hat as it moves along wall)* Oh…oh… oh. *(almost screaming)*. I believe. I believe! I'm sorry I wouldn't sit on your lap!!!! I'll sit on your lap till I'm sixty-three.

(Head comes up over wall. It is an "alien.")

TIMMY. *(jerking head around to audience)* Aaaaaaaaaaa!!! This I don't believe.

ALIEN. Hello. May I come in?

*(**TIMMY** shakes head violently, no.)*

ALIEN. Thank you.

(He goes around and comes in "door.")

May I sit down?

*(**TIMMY** shakes head violently, no.)*

Thank you.

*(He sits on empty stool. So does **TIMMY**. **TIMMY** begins pinching himself.)*

Fascinating. This causes you no pain? It would cause me pain.

TIMMY. I'm trying to wake myself up.

ALIEN. Oh, your species sleeps with its eyes open? Fascinating.

TIMMY. I just look awake. I gotta be asleep because this has to be a dream. I had one last year, and I'm not going to let it happen again.

ALIEN. I am no dream. I am Bilsteep of the planet Wognor. I have come to visit you.

TIMMY. If I give you Reese's pieces, will you leave?

ALIEN. Not until you tell me about Christmas.

TIMMY. Huh?

ALIEN. I have come to find out about Christmas.

TIMMY. That's why you're wearing the Santa Claus hat?

ALIEN. Partly. Also, I know that it is a symbol of a man of good will among your people, and I come in peace.

TIMMY. You came to find out about Christmas?

ALIEN. Partly. It all began many years ago when we saw the colors on your planet.

TIMMY. Colors?

ALIEN. Yes. I must explain. Our eyes are different from yours. We see more colors. Oh, we see red and green and blue, just as you do, but we also see happy.

TIMMY. You mean you see people being happy.

ALIEN. Not exactly. I mean, we can see what people are doing when they are happy, but we can also see happiness itself. It is just like another color for us.

TIMMY. And you saw a lot of people being happy on our planet, on earth?

ALIEN. Well, yes we did, although not that many more than on our own planet. And we saw the dark colors of much sadness, too. But we saw something more.

TIMMY. What?

ALIEN. We do not know. It was a new color. It was much like the color of happiness, but brighter, so much brighter, and somehow different and more beautiful. More beautiful than anything else in the universe. Many years ago we saw this color begin to appear in tiny little spots on your planet. Then, down through the centuries, more and more of the dots appeared, until there were tiny dots of the color like happiness all over your planet.

TIMMY. Why do you need to find out about Christmas?

ALIEN. Because, although there are many tiny dots of the color on your planet at all time of the year, there are far more at Christmas.

TIMMY. Well, lots of people are happy at Christmas.

ALIEN. But this is not the color of happiness. It is so much greater. Tell me what happens at Christmas. *(***READERS 1, 2 & 3** *raise heads.)*

READER 1. So Timmy told him about the dancing Christmas trees.

ALIEN. On Wognor we dress up as Glopglops at harvest time, and this makes us happy, but it could not cause the new color.

READER 2. And Timmy told him about getting the Christmas tree.

ALIEN. When winter comes on Wognor, we cut ludlud bushes and cover them with Tigflad, and this makes us happy, but it could not cause the new color.

READER 3. And Timmy told him about sitting on Santa Claus's lap and getting gifts.

ALIEN. On Wognor we all get gifts on our Gribfoodling day. We are happy, but that could not cause the new color. *(getting excited)* NO! NO! NO! NONE OF THESE THINGS CAN BE THE CAUSE.

TIMMY. Oh, boy. Is Grandma going to be mad at me. I forgot to tell you the most important thing about Christmas.

READER 1. But just when Timmy was about to tell Bilsteep the most important thing about Christmas... .

READER 2. Grandma, and Mom and Dad, who had heard the shouting, came bursting through the door and saw Timmy and Bilsteep....

READER 3. And since they were adults and more mature than Timmy, they all quietly said... . .

READERS 1,2, &3. AAAAAAAAAAAAAAAAAAAAAAAAAARG H!!!!!!!!!!

READER 1. And then Timmy explained and Bilsteep explained....

READER 2. And Timmy's father called the police and argued with them for a long time....

READER 3. And finally the police came over and they called the FBI and argued with them for a long time....

READER 1. And the FBI came over and they called the President and they argued with the President's secretary for a long time....

READER 2. And they all got in cars with Bilsteep to take him to the airport, (**ALIEN** *lowers head*) and about 2:00 A.M. Timmy finally got to bed, but his Mom got him up in the morning to go to school anyhow and they were all sitting at the breakfast table....

READER 3. When Bilsteep walked in looking very dejected.... (**ALIEN** *raises head.*)

TIMMY. Bilsteep....

ALIEN. Greetings.

READER 2. I thought you were on your way to Washington.

ALIEN. I was. But I have only one day on your planet and I must begin my return to Wognor and I shall never return.

READER 2. They let you come back here?

ALIEN. I did not ask them. We were flying over what you call Indiana and I decided to leave them. I think they are searching all over Indiana for pieces of me. They do not know what I can do. They know so little. So many of them are so foolish. I do not understand that color.

TIMMY. You didn't find out what caused the color?

ALIEN. No. They would not answer my questions, only ask their own.

TIMMY. Bilsteep. I'm sorry. I forgot to tell you the most important thing about Christmas.

ALIEN. Then tell me before I must leave. There may still be a chance.

READER 1. So Timmy told Bilsteep the most important thing about Christmas.

READER 2. He told him about Mary and Joseph going to Bethlehem and the birth of the baby Jesus.

READER 3. He told him about the angels telling the shepherds about Jesus' birth.

READER 1. He told him about the wise men coming to bring the baby gifts.

READER 2. And when he forgot something, or got it wrong, Mom or Dad or Grandma helped.

ALIEN. THAT'S IT! THAT'S THE COLOR! It is the color of those who know that God has come to them in the baby.

READER 3. You don't know God on your planet?

ALIEN. We have suspected, but we did not know.

We live our lives on Wognor, but then we die, and we feared that there was nothing more.

Many of you know there is a God who gives you something more.

We try to do what is right on Wognor, but we were never sure that it really mattered.

You know there is a God who sees what you do and that it matters to that God if it is right.

We try to help each other on Wognor. But sometimes we fail and sometimes there is nothing we can do. You know there is a god who can always help you.

READER 3. Sometimes we doubt. Sometimes we aren't sure.

ALIEN. And then your beautiful new color fades. But you have this that we have never had. This God that we only suspected has come to you.

READER 2. But not to you?

ALIEN. Not until now. *(thrilled)*

READER 1. What do you mean?

ALIEN. I see the color in you, in all four of you. You believe now that there is a God and that he has come to you in the child of Bethlehem and in telling the story you have remembered, and that same God is here with you, now. I can see the color on you. *(Others examine their hands.)* No, you cannot see it. But you feel it and you know it and I think you have named it. Happiness is good and it has a good color. But it is nothing like the color I see on you now. It is the color that comes from knowing God has come to you. You call it joy.

READER 3. You said God had not come to Wognor until

now. Will he be born in a manger on Wognor? Or in some other way?

ALIEN. He will come in me. You had the color. You told me the story. I believe. *(Holding out his hands.)* I wish you could see it. It is the most beautiful color in the universe. And it is all over me now. Since you gave me the color, I can return and give it to all on Wognor…who will take it. **(ALIEN** *lowers head.)*

READER 1. And Bilsteep was gone. **(READER 5** *leaves stage.)*

READER 2. But it wasn't over for Timmy and his family. They flew to Washington and they met the President and they were on television and when they got back all Timmy's friends wanted to know about Bilsteep, and then on Christmas Eve, Grandma found Timmy sitting in his room looking very sad.

READER 3. Do you miss Bilsteep?

TIMMY. Well, yeah. A little. But that's not really it.

READER 3. Surely you're not still bored. This must have been the most exciting Christmas time you've ever had.

TIMMY. Yeah, but that's the problem. What do I do next year? We go and see the dancing Christmas trees, and we go to the North Pole or something to get a Christmas tree, and I get to wear my bathrobe and be a shepherd. I'm not sitting on Santa Claus's lap.

GRANDMA. Why was this Christmas so exciting?

TIMMY. Well, gosh, Grandma. When an alien from outer space visits you, that's exciting.

READER 3. Funny. Bilsteep seemed to think there was something else much more exciting.

TIMMY. Yeah, but….Oh, I get it. The really exciting thing about Christmas is that God visited us.

GRANDMA. Yes. As exciting as an alien is, I really think Bilsteep was a lot like us. But when God, who created the whole universe, comes to visit us in Bethlehem…well, that's something really exciting.

TIMMY. Yeah. Not like dancing Christmas trees.

GRANDMA. Very true. Except for one thing. Don't be too hard on your Dad about the dancing Christmas trees and the other things. For your Dad, they're reminders. Things that help him remember. Your Dad's a good Christian, Timmy. Christmas is a very special time when there are all kinds of reminders around that God came to visit us in Bethlehem. I imagine that's why Bilsteep and his people saw more of the special colors on earth at Christmas time. More people were remembering. And partly that's because of dancing Christmas trees and church pageants. Of course, we can remember God came to visit us at any time, but some of the things we do at Christmas help.

TIMMY. So Christmas should always be exciting because it reminds us of the most exciting thing that ever happened in the world.

READER 3. Yes. Except for one thing. I think that when we remember God came to visit us...He comes again.

TIMMY. You mean right now? Right in my room?

READER 3. If you remember hard enough.

(Silence for a moment)

TIMMY. I think He's here.

GRANDMA. I think so too.

TIMMY. *(after a pause)* Grandma. I wish Bilsteep was here... to see what a neat color we are.

The End